MYSTERY at the JELLYBEAN FACTORY

Written by Fran and Lou Sabin
Illustrated by Irene Trivas

Troll Associates

Library of Congress Cataloging in Publication Data

Sabin, Francene.
    Mystery at the jellybean factory.

    (A Troll easy-to-read mystery)
    Summary: Hoping to join their club, Jane tells
the Maple Street Six she has witnessed a robbery,
but because it is April Fools' Day, she is not
believed.
    [1. Robbers and outlaws—Fiction. 2. Clubs—
Fiction. 3. April Fools' Day—Fiction] I. Sabin,
Louis. II. Trivas, Irene, ill. III. Title.
IV. Series: Troll easy-to-read mystery.
PZ7.S1172My   [Fic]   81-10388
ISBN 0-89375-600-8   AACR2
ISBN 0-89375-601-6 (pbk.)

10   9   8   7   6   5   4   3   2   1

Eddie

Sam

Sue

Annie

Mike

Sarah

the
Maple Street Six

The Maple Street Six is the best club in the whole world. That is why I wanted to join. And that is what I told the kids at a special meeting of the club.

"I think Jane is too young," said
Sarah.

Sarah is president of the club. She is
also my big sister. Some sister!

"Sarah is right," Mike agreed. "We
don't want any little kids around."

"Anyway, we are the Maple Street *Six*," Sue told me. "If we let you join, we will have to change the name on the clubhouse door."

MAPLE STREET SIX

"But Jane is a real smart kid," said
Sam.

"And she isn't afraid of anything,"
said Annie.

"Let's take a vote," Eddie said.

I stood outside while the kids voted.
Sarah came out. She gave me the bad
news.

Two kids voted *yes*. Four kids voted *no*.

"You have to do something special to get into our club," Sarah told me. "Maybe when you're older . . ."

I wanted to kick her. But I was also starting to cry, and I didn't want her to see. I ran home.

The next morning my mother sent me
to the store.

"Milk, bread, and peanut butter," I
sang as I walked. I always do that so I
won't forget what to buy.

"Milk, bread, and peanut butter." I
was almost at the store.

"Milk, bread, and—Holy smoke!"
Across the street there was a bank.
Two men wearing masks came running
out.

They threw two big bags into the back
of the truck. Then one man ran back into
the bank. The other man stood on the
sidewalk. He was waving a gun.

There were lots of people around.
They had their hands in the air.
The men were robbing the bank!

Boy, I thought, if I could stop those guys — that would be something special! Then the Maple Streeters would *beg* me to join their silly old club.

Nobody was watching me. So I jumped into the back of the truck. I hid behind the bags.

The robbers threw in two more bags. I ducked way down. It was dark in there. They didn't see me. They shut the doors.

The truck began moving. Fast. Faster. I slid all around the back. So did the money bags. It was really scary.

The truck went screeching around a corner. I fell and banged my head on the floor.

Before I could stop myself, I yelled, "Ow!"

"What's that?" one of the robbers asked.

I started to shake. What if they found me?

"It's nothin'," the other guy said. "Keep drivin'. It's your nerves."

At last the truck stopped. I squeezed way back in a corner. The doors opened. Each robber grabbed a bag. I heard them walk away. Then a door slammed.

This was my chance. I peeked outside. There was a big building, with dirty windows, and a bunch of barrels and boxes. No people.

I climbed out and ran behind the barrels—just in time.

The robbers came out of the building.

"This warehouse is a good place to hide the loot," one of the men said.

"Yeah. We'll come back later and get it," the other one said.

They carried the rest of the bags into the building.

Then they got into the truck and drove away.

Now it was time for *my* getaway. I had to go to the clubhouse—and *fast!*

I'll get the Maple Streeters, I thought, and bring them back here. Here? *What is this place, anyway?*

I ran around the building. Then I saw a sign. It said: THE FROGBOTTOM BUBBLE GUM AND JELLYBEAN COMPANY WAREHOUSE.

I ran a few blocks. Then I got tired and sat down to rest.

"Oh," I groaned. "I can't run all the way across town. It's much too far."

I saw a big red bus. It was the same one that goes by my house. I wished I had money for the fare. Then I remembered—"Milk, bread, and peanut butter." I did have money!

I waved at the bus. It stopped, and I got on.

The bus came to my street. I jumped
off and ran to the clubhouse of the Maple
Street Six.

I ran inside. All the kids were there.

"Wait till you hear what happened to me!" I shouted.

"You saw the Seven Dwarfs," Annie said.

"You flew to the moon," Eddie said.

"You found a million dollars," Sue said.

"You found tons and tons of candy and bubble gum," Sam said.

He smiled and licked his lips. Sam really likes food—especially candy.

"Money *and* candy," I told them. "And you have to help me catch two robbers."

"Oh, come on, Jane. We know today is April Fools' Day," Sarah said.

"You can't fool us," Mike said.

"It's not very funny, either," Annie said.

I started to sniffle. "Honest, this is no April Fools' joke. I followed two bank robbers. I know where they hid the loot. I mean, the money from the bank."

Sarah stared at me for a long time. Then she said, "I can tell when Jane is joking. She's telling the truth now."

"Okay, let's hear the whole thing," Sue said.

"Specially about the candy," Sam said.

Everybody sat in a circle. I stood in the middle. I told them everything that had happened.

Mike jumped up. "Let's get to the warehouse," he said.

"Lunch first. I'm starved," Sam begged.

"Milk, bread, and peanut butter. I almost forgot!" I said.

Sarah held up her hand. "All right, gang. First, we'll buy the food," she said. "Then we can all eat at my house."

And we hurried out of the clubhouse.

We ate the world's fastest lunch. Even Sam ate fast. Then we zipped to the bus stop.

"Do you know where to get off?" Eddie asked me.

"I don't know the name of the street," I said. "But I remember there was a big statue of a man with a sword on a horse."

The bus came, and we piled on.

We watched out the windows for the statue. After a ride that seemed to take forever, Eddie yelled, "There it is!"

The bus came to a stop. We jumped
off.

"Follow me," I called.

I led them right to THE
FROGBOTTOM BUBBLE GUM AND
JELLYBEAN COMPANY WAREHOUSE.

"Is the whole place filled with candy?" Sam asked hopefully.

"It must be. But we came for the money," Annie said.

"Oh, well," Sam sighed.

Sarah walked to the door. "Is this where the robbers went?" she asked.

"Yes. But I guess it's locked," I said.

Eddie tried the doorknob. It turned. The door opened.

"Come on," he whispered.

We tiptoed into the warehouse.

It was gloomy. And big. Very, very big.

"Where's the money?" asked Sue.

I shook my head. "I don't know. We have to hunt for it."

"That's my kind of hunting. Oh, yum," said Sam.

He was looking at blue bubble-gum boxes, piled all the way to the roof. And at huge brown sacks of jellybeans. And at yellow boxes marked CHOCOLATE-COVERED MARSHMALLOWS. And at barrels of big, salted pretzels.

"Come here!" called Sarah.

We rushed over. She pointed to a pile
of sacks. They were gray and had dollar
signs printed on them.

"Those are the ones!" I cried.

Eddie grabbed a sack. He tried to pick
it up.

"Ohhhhh! This weighs a ton. I can't
lift it," he puffed.

"We need the police," Mike said.

So Annie and Eddie and Sue went to
get the police. Sarah and Sam and Mike
and I stayed in the warehouse. We
guarded the money.

After a while, we heard the door open.

"They're back," I said.

"*Sssh!*" Mike whispered. "Listen to the footsteps. It's just one person."

I peeked around some boxes—and leaped back.

"It's one of the robbers," I whispered.

As quickly as we could, we climbed over some barrels and hid behind a lot of big brown sacks that were piled on boxes. Then we scrunched down and waited.

The robber walked right to the money. He picked up a bag. Just then, Sam's box began to rock back and forth. He slipped and fell against two huge sacks.

CRUNCH!

The sacks fell right on the robber. They split open. Millions of jellybeans poured over him.

He couldn't move. All you could see was his head. The rest was a mountain of jellybeans. Yellow ones. Red ones. Pink ones. And green ones. It was beautiful.

The warehouse door opened again. This time it was Annie and Eddie and Sue. Right behind them came two police officers. The other robber was handcuffed to one of them. The police had grabbed him outside the warehouse.

"Here we are," I called. "By the big candy mountain."

Everyone was quite impressed when they saw the robber we'd trapped.

"Good job, kids," said one of the officers.

"You thought we were pulling an April Fools' joke on you," Annie said.

The officer's face turned red. "Only at first. But then we realized you were serious," he said.

The police handcuffed the other robber and marched both of them to the door.

"By the way, kids," one of the officers
said. "You'll get a nice reward for
catching these guys."

"A reward? Wow!" Sue cheered.

"That's great," Mike said.

"I know how we can spend some of it," Sarah said. She was wearing a big smile.

"How?" I asked.

"On a new sign for the clubhouse. It will say **THE MAPLE STREET SEVEN**," she said.

All the kids were grinning at me.

"We have to make it official," said Annie.

"Okay, how many want Jane in the club?" asked Eddie. He counted five hands.

"Who didn't vote?" he asked.

We looked around. There was Annie and Sue and Mike and Eddie and Sarah and me. Where was Sam?

"There he is," said Sarah.

She pointed to the jellybean
mountain. It was a smaller mountain now
—with Sam in the middle of it.

"I vote for Jane, too," he said, between mouthfuls of jellybeans.

Now that it was official, we all joined Sam on the jellybean mountain. And that's how the Maple Street Six became the Maple Street Seven!